LOVE LETTERS TO MY BELOVED

MARLENE DECOOK

Copyright © 2024 by Marlene Decook

ISBN: 979-8-89397-336-5

Edition: First

Published by Elite Scribes Book Writing

TABLE OF CONTENTS

Searching For My Love 7

If You Only Knew 8

Just Knock On My Door 9

Taste My Love 10

My Love, My Love. I'll Wait For You. 11

When You're Not With Me 12

I Want The World To Know 13

Chasing You Through A Time Zone 14

My Imagination Of Loving You 15

You're In My Head 16

My Beating Heart 17

Lost Without You 18

My Empty Bed 19

The Little Star 20

Missing You 21

I Want You 22

My Love 23

Long Distance Love 24

My Memories Of You.. 25

He Doesn't Even Know Me.................................. 26

Before you begin, play **Very Sad** by **Enchan** to uncover the mood behind the words.

Marlene Decook

SEARCHING FOR MY LOVE

I've searched for you crossing land and sea and oceans. I've crossed the desert far and wide; I've gone through the heavens and hell. Where are you, my love? Must I dream you to come true? I need you, and I won't rest till you see my heart and soul. I love you and I will search far and wide, far and through.

As I walk beyond a grass of trails, I see a bench, and I sit to rest. The smell of a garden of flowers is where you are. I see you walk so gracefully. And my eyes can't believe it's you. Your smile melts my heart, and we talk. We walk together, and like magic and magnets, we are bound—forever, my love.

I will love you and only you. ♥

IF YOU ONLY KNEW

If you only knew how much I've loved you. The years are like small moments — I want to love you forever. I can't live or function without you. You bring the best out of me, you can't do no wrong in my eyes because you are part of me. You're a gentle soul who should be loved, and I love you as the heavens already know.

Stay with me, my love, for I will teach you the greatest love of all. When I touch you, my heart skips a beat because you're the happiness that makes me shine. I love you, and I will cherish you for a lifetime.

Loving you, my sweetness, forever and ever. 

JUST KNOCK ON MY DOOR

If I could touch your hand, I would. If I could kiss your lips, I would. If I could whisper in your ear to tell you how much you mean to me, I would. If I could tell you how much I love you, I would. Come back to me, my love. I miss you. If I could, I'd knock on every door. But I will wait and give you the time that you need and let you figure out—that one day, you will know that it was me who truly loved you. And when you realize how much I care, my doors will always be open for you, my love. I wait for your return. I love you, my darling. Just come back to me. I will always be here for you.

Your true love, waiting. 🖤 🖤

TASTE MY LOVE

When I say that I love you and I want you, I mean that from the bottom of my heart. I've pulled these words out as if I was taking water out of a deep well. And I give that love to the person that I've fallen in love with. I am the one who will quench that thirst, and you'll always know where it came from.

My love for you is as true as the water that you will receive. I look into your beautiful eyes and have no regrets. I have looked at your precious lips as you drink my water that you received, and I'm longing to kiss your lips so I may seal this love forever. You are so precious, and I love you more than words could ever express.

I love you forever. 🖤🖤

MY LOVE, MY LOVE, I'LL WAIT FOR YOU

You'll never know the amount of love that I have for you and, most of all, how long I've carried it in my heart for you. I wish I could be with you and let my love pour out like the gentle spring raindrops that feel so refreshing on the skin. The softness of the breeze that flows against your skin will be my gentle touch.

I want to rub your chest with my hands and stroke your hair between my fingers. And to smell your skin because it belongs to you—and only you. You are the only thing that will put a smile on my face and give my heart a rest from missing you so much. The only ones who know how much I miss you are the angels who are guarding me from falling apart. They tell me that you're not far behind and that you love me in return.

I love you, my love. XOXO 🖤 🖤 🖤

WHEN YOU'RE NOT WITH ME

As the days turn into nights, and the days turn into weeks and months, my heart grows fonder of you, and my love for you becomes the foundation of our lives together.

And I need you, my love, to fill this house with joy and laughter and to give me the sunshine that I crave every day. I love you more each day. And I need to kiss your tender lips, and to caress your beautiful body, and to fill my heart next to yours.

I am lost without you, and I can become a mess when you're away too long. It's your love that shines through like a light from the heavens, and the sound of beautiful music to bring a nice smile to my face. Yes, my love, this is what you do to me when you aren't around.

I love you endlessly. 🖤 🖤 🖤

I WANT THE WORLD TO KNOW

If I could describe my love for you, it would be drawn on many walls, even on the streets. And I'd write it on the clouds so the world could see and feel the love that I have for you.

Will you see me acting like I'm drunk? I am... I'm drunk on your love for me.

I cry when I don't know where you are. I have to look for you in every corner of the world. And when I see you—I put a smile on my face; my heart becomes calm, like the sea when it's told to be calm. That is what your beautiful love and soul do to me because I love you so. 🖤 🖤 🖤

CHASING YOU THROUGH A TIME ZONE

When I sit and think about it, it brings me great pleasure and happiness. It is you who I have followed in the back of my mind, as I've done for a lifetime.

It's true that you don't know me, and yet I know you. I've loved you forever. And I've kissed you a million times. We've laughed together and cried together, and we've made love together.

I can breathe the same air as you because you live in me. And I will always chase you in my head because it's all about my memories that I created for you and I. Your home is in my heart, and I love you living there with me. I love you, my dearest Angel, because you love me too. 🖤 🖤 🖤

MY IMAGINATION OF LOVING YOU

Oh, how I want to sit next to you on a train or a bus and travel by your side. And to enjoy those miles with you. I know we are strangers. But the very thought of you next to me makes me smile and flutter with good energy. And for those moments that will turn into hours, maybe days, I don't know your destination; I only know that when I laid eyes on you, you were mine. I feel for you, and we have never spoken a word. Simply... a glance that stole my heart and took my breath away. My heart wanted to grab your soul and tell you that you were mine. But I didn't because I was afraid of rejection. I just wanted to let my head rest upon your shoulder, and then I would've been in a magical world of my own with you in it, my love. 🖤 🖤 🖤

YOU'RE IN MY HEAD

I don't have you in my life the way I'd love to have you, and yet, in my mind, I make you up into the man that I want and need. I walk on many trails in the woods, and beyond the trees, I see you just ahead. And I pretend that is you.

I put every aspect of you into the man that I want. And it starts at the heart. And it ends with how you will love me and your amazing thoughts of me in your mind. And I see myself running up to you and telling you to hold my hand as I reach out to yours. Your smile is all I need to see because it tells me with a nice kiss that you love me.

I love you, my love, and I'll love you forever. 🤍🤍🤍

MY BEATING HEART

Like the rivers flowing into the deep ocean, my love for you flows in the same manner. I'm looking for the perfect time and place to share this beautiful love song just for you. And if you love it back, then we can mingle together and share an amazing experience of all that our hearts have held back for so long. The void that you have been trying to fill will finally be filled with only one person that you will love forever.

And if you let go, you will crush the very heart that beats in your chest. I love you, my dearest heart, so please don't ever let me go. I will love you forever. And I will keep you safe in my heart.

Loving you, my love, is all I want. 🖤 🖤 🖤

LOST WITHOUT YOU

I'm lost without you, and I feel so much loneliness. I'll look for you like a lost puppy dog. And when I do find you, my heart will beat with so much happiness. Just the sight of you will ease all that I've been through because I can't live without you. I know I'll find you, and when I do, I won't stop holding you.

Yes, I will climb the hills, and I will look in every corner of the earth. Just for you, my dear heart, and once I find you, I will never let you go. I'll love you till the end of time and walk with you hand in hand. I'll always be by your side, and you'll never let me go because of my love for you.

Kisses and hugs for you, my sweet, loving husband. For no one could take your place. I love you so, so much. ♥ ♥ ♥

MY EMPTY BED

As I lay in my bed, I think of you day and night. Not a moment of rest, with the thought of you, goes unnoticed by my heart that speaks of love for you.

Will you ever come to me?

Or must I miss you like the deserts miss the rains?

The scent of you always brings me back to you. I wish to hold you between my arms and never let you go. These tears have me feeling so empty because you're not here with me. I love you and I would wait a lifetime just for you. So, hurry and come back to me. I'm cold, and I need your warmth.

You are the one my heart beats for. 🖤 🖤 🖤

THE LITTLE STAR

To love you on the highest level, is the same as all the brilliant stars that shine through the night. It's there for all to see. There is truth when you look into my eyes. My love for you comes like the waters that flow from any direction that the oceans can see. I long for you to love me in the same way. And to cherish me like no other love that you have known.

I could never hurt you. I can only love you. When I tap on a shoulder, and I think that it's you, it's only because I'm missing you and looking for you. When I'm alone, I think of only you. I wish to hold you and never let you go.

Loving you always, your little star. 🖤 🖤 🖤

MISSING YOU

Must I beg you for your love? I wait for you to tell me how you have missed me. I don't want to beg, but my heart cries for your tender touch, your tender kisses. I long to be between your strong arms and to cuddle and lay my head on your chest. And to listen to the beautiful sound of your heartbeat. May your heart beat only for me. I want to hold you near to me and whisper pure, sweet words into your ears. I want to love you, hold you close, and make a home for you in my heart. Darling, don't make me wait too long. The pain of loving you so long is the price I've paid.

I love you. Be with me and never let me go. 🖤 🖤 🖤

I WANT YOU

I want to love you, but you're so far away. The distance between us has brought many tears. It has made me jealous. It has torn my heart apart. It has made me doubt. The promises that you have broken have brought many tears. Please tell me, my love, when will it be real? Real of us. Us to meet and to love. The distance has me wondering if you want to be loved.

I've given you my heart and soul. I promise to love you forever, my love. All you have to do is come into existence and make it real. I promise you won't regret the love from me. I will take away all your fears. And you will see that my love is true. I love you so much, my darling.

Take me into your arms and love me. 🖤 🖤 🖤

MY LOVE

When I think of you, I close my eyes and smile. You have given me many years of happiness. When I was hungry, you fed me; when I was sick, you were there. No matter what the need was, you were there.

I have never known a love such as you. You loved me as if I were the only person on this planet. And I was so amazed by your beautiful soul. I have never met anyone such as you. You took me under your wing before we fell in love. And you showed me the meaning of true love. I have fallen hard for you and loved you back. I loved you so much that I want it to last forever. You're the best, and I'll love you forever.

Your lover forever. 🖤 🖤 🖤

LONG DISTANCE LOVE

I wait patiently for your arrival, yet it seems like a lifetime. I know that crossing the oceans is wild and dangerous. I can only pray for your journey to be calm and safe. I love you, and may the angels protect you. Since I last saw you, your last words to me were that you would come back in two months. And to wait for you.

My love, it's been a whole year. How can I know if you were on that journey to come back to me? I need to know if I still have a place in your heart. My love, if we should meet again, I would be more happier than the angels in heaven. I'll love you forever. I'll continue to wait for your return.

Your lover, from the heart 🖤 🖤 🖤

MY MEMORIES OF YOU

When I look at you, you're more beautiful than the garden itself. When I see your beautiful smile, it brings me happiness. And when the wind blows your beautiful hair, it's a scene to be admired, and with your dress flowing with the wind, it's so breathtaking. My love, you are so beautiful. I keep a memory of all the times and places we've been. You are the love of my life, my firstborn.

I know that you're an angel now, and you are with me wherever I go. Your memories are the most precious things that I possess, and I carry you always in my heart. Always know that I have loved you since day one.

I will always love you, my darling daughter. Always. 

HE DOESN'T EVEN KNOW ME

He's so beautiful, and I wish that I could just touch his hand or even put a tender kiss on his lips. But I know that I will never ever get the chance to ever stand next to his beautiful soul. Not even a single glance will my eyes ever get; the chance just to gaze at him from a far distance.

I could never compete or compare to the beautiful women that surround him. I'm a plain, simple woman who is in love with him. I want nothing of him, only to be his desire and his only true love. I have nothing else to offer him, only my truest sincerity and my love, respect, and honesty. And my companionship and anything else his heart desires of me.

I give you my endless days and as far as the galaxies can take us together, my love, I am yours forever. And if you should ever send me away from your side, I will always be close by.

If you should call my name, my love, I can only love you and bury myself in this ocean of love that I feel for you, my precious love.